# Kate DiCamillo

# Mercy Watson
## to the Rescue

*illustrated by* Chris Van Dusen

CANDLEWICK PRESS

First paperback edition 2009

The Library of Congress has cataloged the hardcover edition as follows:

DiCamillo, Kate.
Mercy Watson to the rescue / Kate DiCamillo ; illustrated by Chris Van Dusen.
—1st ed.
p.   cm.
Summary:  After Mercy the pig snuggles to sleep with the Watsons,
all three awaken with the bed teetering on the edge of a big hole in the floor.
ISBN 978-0-7636-2270-1 (hardcover)
[1. Pigs—Fiction.  2. Neighbors—Fiction.  3. Fire departments—Fiction.
4. Humorous stories.]    I. Van Dusen, Chris, ill.
PZ7.D54146Me  2005
[Fic]—dc22      2004051896

978-0-7636-4504-5 (paperback)

10 11 12 13 14 CCP 10 9 8 7 6 5 4 3

Printed in Shenzhen, Guangdong, China

This book was typeset in Mrs. Eaves.
The illustrations were done in gouache.

Candlewick Press
99 Dover Street
Somerville, Massachusetts 02144

visit us at www.candlewick.com

*For Alison McGhee, who likes her toast
with a great deal of butter*

**K. D.**


*For Guggy with love*

**C. V.**

# Chapter
# 1

Mr. Watson and Mrs. Watson have a pig named Mercy.

Each night, they sing Mercy to sleep.

*"Bright, bright is the morning sun,"* sing Mr. and Mrs. Watson,

*"but brighter still is our darling one.*

*Dark, dark is the coming night,*

*but oh, our Mercy shines so bright."*

This song makes Mercy feel warm inside, as if she has just eaten hot toast with a great deal of butter on it.

Mercy likes hot toast with a great deal of butter on it.

But when Mr. and Mrs. Watson kiss her good night and turn off the light, Mercy's room becomes dark.

Very dark.

And Mercy does not feel warm and
buttery-toasty inside anymore.
She feels afraid.

One night, after Mr. and Mrs. Watson sang their song about the sun, kissed Mercy good night, and turned off the light, Mercy decided something. She decided that she would be much happier if she wasn't sleeping alone. And so Mercy got out of her bed

and went and got in bed with Mr. and
Mrs. Watson.

She snuggled up between them.

Mercy felt warm inside, as if she had
just eaten hot toast with a great deal of
butter on it.

# Chapter
## 2

Mr. Watson and Mrs. Watson and
Mercy were all in bed together.

They were all dreaming.

Mr. Watson was dreaming of driving
a very fast car.

*"Vrooomm,"* said Mr. Watson in his
sleep. *"Vroom, vrooomm."*

Mrs. Watson was dreaming of
buttering hot toast for Mercy.
   She buttered one piece and then
another piece and then another.

 7

"Have some more, dear," Mrs.
Watson said in her sleep. "Eat up,
yum, yum."

Mercy was dreaming about hot
buttered toast, too.

8

In Mercy's dream, hot buttered toast was piled high on her favorite blue plate and Mrs. Watson was buttering still more.

It was an excellent dream.

Mr. Watson said, *"Vroom, vroom."*

Mrs. Watson said, "Have some more, dear."

Mercy snuffled and chewed in her sleep.

Mr. Watson and Mrs. Watson and Mercy were all so busy sleeping that they did not hear the bed creak.

They were all so busy dreaming that they did not hear the floor moan.

Chapter

3

# BOOM!

A hole opened under the Watsons'

bed. **CRACK!**

The Watsons' bed fell into the hole.

Mr. Watson woke up.

Mrs. Watson woke up.

Mercy woke up, too.

"What the —?" said Mr. Watson.

"Oink?" said Mercy.

"It's an earthquake!" shouted Mrs. Watson. "It's the end of the world!"

"Nonsense," said Mr. Watson, but he did not sound very sure.

He sounded frightened.

Mercy, however, was not frightened.

Mercy was hungry.

"Oink?" said Mercy again.

She moved to the end of the bed.

BOOM!

CRACK!

14

The bed fell a little farther into the hole in the floor.

"Don't move," shouted Mr. Watson. "Whatever you do, don't move!"

Mr. Watson and Mrs. Watson and Mercy held very still.

Mrs. Watson started to cry.

"I know exactly what we must do," said Mr. Watson. "We must call the fire department. They will rescue us."

"But you said we should not move," said Mrs. Watson. "How can we call the fire department if we cannot move?"

Mercy recalled her lovely toast-filled dream.

She wondered if there was any toast in the kitchen.

While Mr. Watson and Mrs. Watson were arguing, Mercy hopped off the bed.

"Look!" said Mrs. Watson. "Mercy has escaped."

"She is going to find help," said Mr. Watson. "She is going to alert the fire department."

Mercy left the bedroom at a gallop.

She was in a hurry.

She was on her way to the kitchen.

She was looking for some toast.

# Chapter
# 4

In the kitchen, Mercy sniffed the table.

She sniffed the kitchen counters.

She sniffed the floor.

But there was no toast.

There was not even a crumb of toast.

Mercy's stomach growled in disappointment.

# BOOM! CRACK!

"Help us!" Mrs. Watson called.

Mercy thought very hard.

Where could she get a snack?

And the answer came to her.

Baby Lincoln always had sugar cookies.

Baby Lincoln lived next door.

And Baby Lincoln liked to share.

Mercy took the kitchen doorknob in her mouth.

She turned it.

"Help!" Mrs. Watson called again.

*Sugar cookies,* thought Mercy.

She stepped outside.

# Chapter 5

The Lincoln Sisters live next door to the Watsons.

Eugenia Lincoln is the older sister. She has many opinions.

One of Eugenia's opinions is that pigs should not live in houses.

Eugenia often says, "Listen closely to

me, Baby. Pigs are farm animals. They belong on farms. They do not belong in houses."

"Yes, Sister," says Baby.

Baby Lincoln is the younger sister.

She is the baby of the family.

Baby agrees with everything Eugenia says.

It is easier that way.

But secretly, Baby has an opinion of her own.

Baby's opinion is that Mercy is good company.

At the Lincoln Sisters' house, Mercy looked into Baby's window.

She could see Baby sleeping.

Mercy pressed her snout up against the windowpane.

"Oink," said Mercy.

But Baby did not hear her.

"Snuffle," said Mercy.

But Baby did not wake up.

Mercy tapped her hoof against the window.

Baby sat up in bed.

"Who's there?" she said.

28

Baby saw Mercy's snout pressed up against the window.

"A monster!" shouted Baby. "A monster at my window!"

Mercy shook her head.

"Sister!" shouted Baby. "Help, help, a monster!"

Eugenia woke up.

She did not put in her teeth.

She did not put on her glasses.

Eugenia went straight to the phone and called the fire department.

"There is a crisis of an uncertain

nature at 52 Deckawoo Drive," said
Eugenia Lincoln. "Come
immediately."

And then Eugenia put on her robe
and rushed to Baby's room.

In her own opinion, Eugenia
Lincoln was very good in a crisis.

# Chapter
# 6

What is going on in here?" asked Eugenia.

"There's a monster outside," said Baby. She pointed at the window.

"That is not a monster," said Eugenia. "*That* is the *pig* from next door."

"Mercy?" said Baby.

Eugenia shook her fist.

"In my opinion," said Eugenia, "pigs belong on farms."

"Yes, Sister," said Baby.

Eugenia tapped a knuckle against the window.

"Get out of my yard!" she shouted at Mercy.

"Oh, Sister," said Baby. "Don't yell at her. You'll hurt her feelings."

"She doesn't have feelings," shouted Eugenia. "She's a *pig*!"

"Oh," said Baby, "I'm sure you're wrong, dear."

"I am not wrong!" Eugenia shouted. "I'm never wrong. I know a pig when I see one!"

Eugenia scowled. She pressed her nose against the windowpane.

Mercy stared at Eugenia.

Eugenia stared at Mercy.

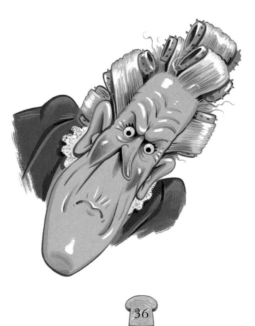

*"Pig!"* shouted Eugenia.

She turned and ran out of Baby's room.

"Oh, dear," said Baby Lincoln. "Oh, my."

# Chapter
# 7

Eugenia ran toward Mercy.

Mercy's heart beat faster.

There was going to be a chase!

Mercy loved a chase.

She let Eugenia get very close to her.

"Oink!" said Mercy, dashing away.

"Get out of my yard!" shouted
Eugenia.

"Oink-oink!" said Mercy.

She ran in circles.

She kicked up her heels.

"*No — pigs — allowed!*"

Eugenia shouted.

"Oh, Sister," said Baby.

"Please be careful."

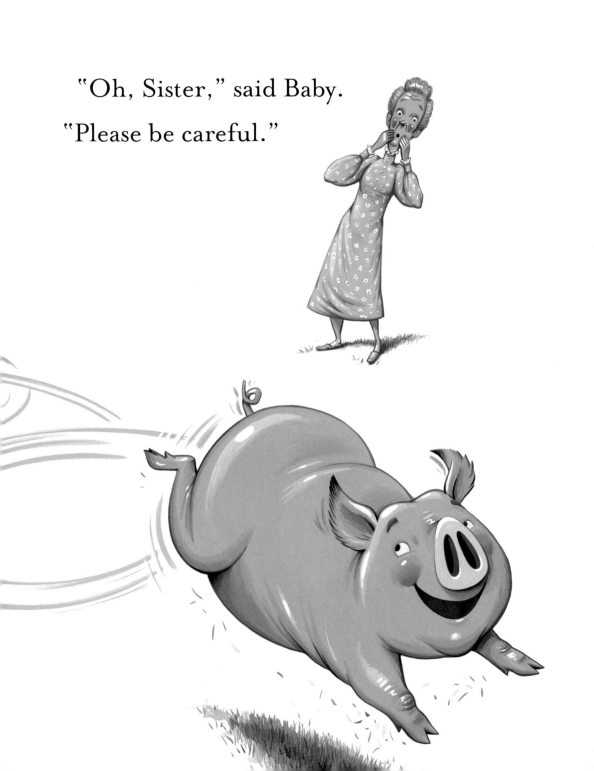

A siren wailed.

A fire truck pulled into the Lincoln Sisters' driveway.

Ned and Lorenzo got out of the truck.

"Do you think that's the emergency?" Ned asked.

"Could be," said Lorenzo.

Ned and Lorenzo sighed.

"You never know with this job," said Lorenzo.

"You're right," said Ned. "You never know."

# Chapter
# 8

Ma'am," said Lorenzo to Baby, "did you call the fire department?"

"Oh, dear," said Baby. "I did not. But Eugenia may have called."

"Who is Eugenia?" asked Ned.

"My sister," said Baby.

"Is that her?" asked Lorenzo. "The one chasing the pig?"

"Yes," said Baby. "That's her."

Baby and Ned and Lorenzo watched Eugenia chasing Mercy through the yard.

Lorenzo cleared his throat.

"What was the emergency exactly?" asked Ned.

"I thought I saw a monster at my bedroom window," said Baby. "But it was not a monster. It was Mercy."

"Mercy?" said Lorenzo.

"The pig," said Baby. "The pig who lives next door."

"I see," said Ned.

"Eugenia does not care for Mercy," said Baby. "In her opinion, pigs belong on farms."

"There's something to be said for that opinion," said Lorenzo.

Ned nodded.

"Help!" shouted a faraway voice. "Help, help! Help us!"

"Did you hear that?" asked Ned.

"Somebody is in trouble," said Lorenzo. "Let's go."

# Chapter
# 9

Ned and Lorenzo ran toward the call for help.

They went into the Watsons' house.

"HELP!"

Ned and Lorenzo looked up.

They saw a bed hanging out of the ceiling.

They saw Mr. and Mrs. Watson holding on to the bed for dear life.

"We are saved!" cried Mrs. Watson.

"Of course we are saved," said Mr. Watson. "Mercy has alerted the fire department."

"She is amazing!" said Mrs. Watson. "She is unbelievable!"

"She is a *porcine wonder!*" said Mr. Watson.

Ned and Lorenzo ran upstairs. They picked up Mr. and Mrs. Watson.

The Watsons' bed sighed loudly and crashed all the way through the floor.

Mr. Watson looked at the hole where
the bed used to be.

"I have always believed very firmly in the fire department," said Mr. Watson.

"As have I," said Mrs. Watson. "As have I."

From outside the Watsons' house came a squeal.

"Gotcha!" shouted Eugenia.

# Chapter
# 10

Ned and Lorenzo and Mr. and Mrs. Watson all went outside.

Eugenia was sitting on the ground.

Her arms were wrapped around Mercy's neck.

Her cheek was resting on Mercy's back.

Eugenia was breathing very loudly.

"This pig," she said, "was on my property."

"We'd prefer that you did not call her a pig," said Mrs. Watson.

"We would prefer that you call her a *porcine wonder*," said Mr. Watson. "After all, she did save us. She's a hero."

"She's a *pig*," said Eugenia.

She started to cry.

"There, there, Sister," said Baby.

She bent over and patted Eugenia on the back.

Mercy yawned.

She was very tired.

"I guess that's it," said Ned.

"Yep," said Lorenzo. "Our work here is done."

"Wait," said Mrs. Watson. "It's almost time for breakfast."

"Oink?" asked Mercy.

"That's right. Breakfast," said
Mrs. Watson.

She kissed the top of Mercy's head.

She looked up at the firemen.

"Do you boys like toast?"

# Chapter
# 11

In the Watsons' house, around the Watsons' kitchen table, sat Eugenia Lincoln and Baby Lincoln and Mr. Watson and Mrs. Watson and Ned and Lorenzo.

And Mercy, of course.

She was at the head of the table, in the seat of honor.

And in front of her, on her favorite
blue plate, was a very tall stack of hot
buttered toast.

"A toast to Mercy," said Mr. Watson,
holding up his glass of orange juice.

"A toast to our darling, our dear,"
said Mrs. Watson.

"A toast to Mercy," said Baby.

"In my opinion," said Eugenia, "pigs should not be toasted. In my opinion, pigs do not belong at the kitchen table."

"To our hero," said Mr. Watson. "Where would we be without Mercy?"

"Yes," said Mrs. Watson. "Who would have saved us?"

"I can't imagine," said Ned.

"Me neither," said Lorenzo.

They all clinked glasses.

Mercy had another piece of toast.

# Chapter
# 12

Outside the Watsons' house, the sun was rising.

First the sun was red.

And then it was orange.

It rose higher and higher.

Inside the Watsons' house, Mercy was lying on the couch.

She was getting ready to take a nap.

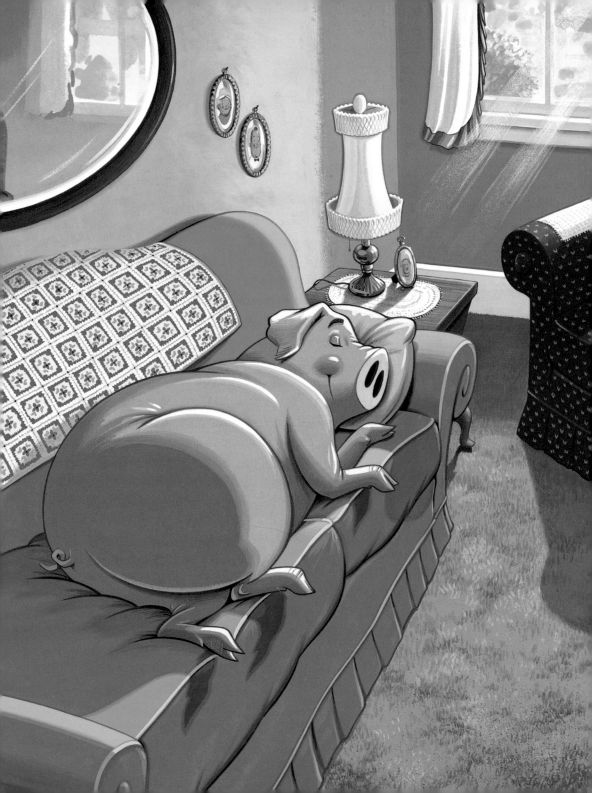

*"Bright, bright is the morning sun,"*

sang Mr. and Mrs. Watson together,

*"but brighter still is our porcine wonder. . . ."*

Mercy smiled.

She closed her eyes.

She was asleep before Mr. and Mrs.

Watson even finished the song.

Kate DiCamillo is the renowned author of numerous books for young readers, including all of the Mercy Watson stories. About *Mercy Watson to the Rescue,* she says, "Mercy Watson had been in my head for a long time, but I couldn't figure out how to tell her story. One day, my friend Alison was going on and on and on about the many virtues of toast. As I listened to her, I could see Mercy nodding in emphatic agreement. Sometimes you don't truly understand a character until you know what she loves above all else." Kate DiCamillo lives in Minneapolis.

**Chris Van Dusen** is the author-illustrator of *Down to the Sea with Mr. Magee*, *A Camping Spree with Mr. Magee*, *If I Built a Car*, and *The Circus Ship*. He says, "When I first read *Mercy Watson to the Rescue*, the characters were very vivid in my mind, and they just came to life when I started painting. This is exactly the type of story I love to illustrate — a wonderfully silly adventure with lots of action." Chris Van Dusen lives in Maine.

Join Mercy Watson

in all six of her pig tales!